The Three Billy Goats Gruff

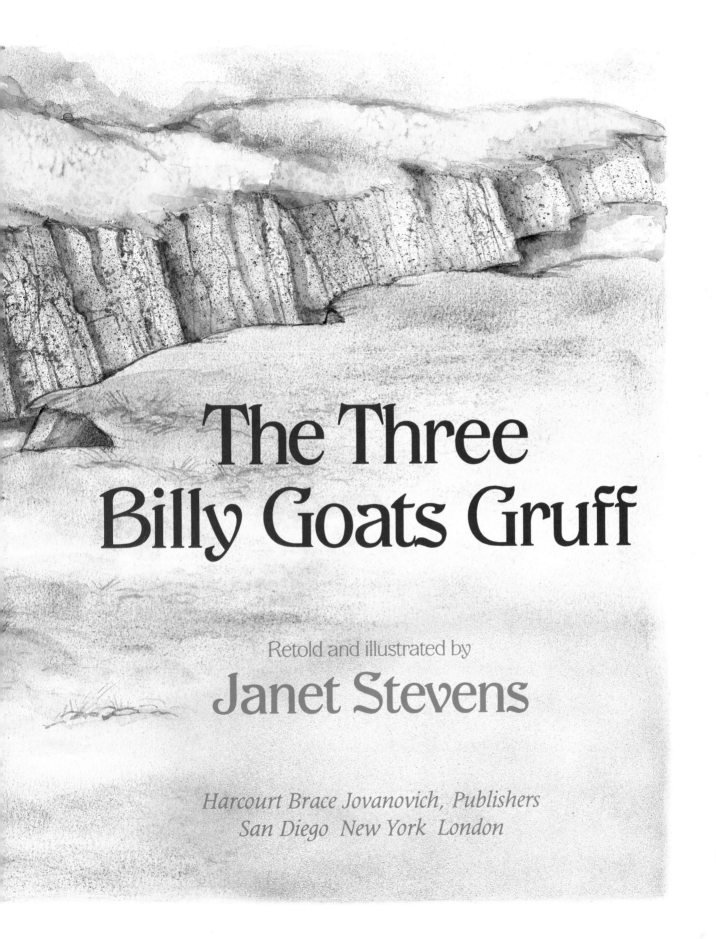

The Three
Billy Goats Gruff

Retold and illustrated by

Janet Stevens

Harcourt Brace Jovanovich, Publishers
San Diego New York London

Requests for permission to make copies of any
part of the work should be mailed to:
Permissions, Harcourt Brace Jovanovich, Publishers,
Orlando, Florida 32887.

Library of Congress Cataloging-in-Publication Data
Stevens, Janet.
The three Billy Goats Gruff.
Summary: Three clever billy goats outwit a big,
ugly troll that lives under the bridge they must
cross on their way up the mountain.
[1. Fairy tales. 2. Folklore—Norway] I. Title.
PZ8.S614Th 1987   398.2'45297358'09481 [E]   86-33512
ISBN 0-15-286396-6

First edition

A B C D E

The paintings in this book were done in watercolor, colored pencil, and pastel,
on Strathmore Bristol board.
The text type was set in Meridien and the display type was set in Floreal Haas.
Composition by Thompson Type, San Diego, California
Printed and bound by Tien Wah Press, Singapore
Production supervision by Warren Wallerstein and Rebecca Miller
Designed by Nancy Ponichtera

For Judy Volc – thanks for giving me the OK
And for the goats at Stone Mountain Petting Zoo

Once upon a time there were three billy goats and their name was Gruff. They ate the grass in their valley until it was all gone. And they were hungry.

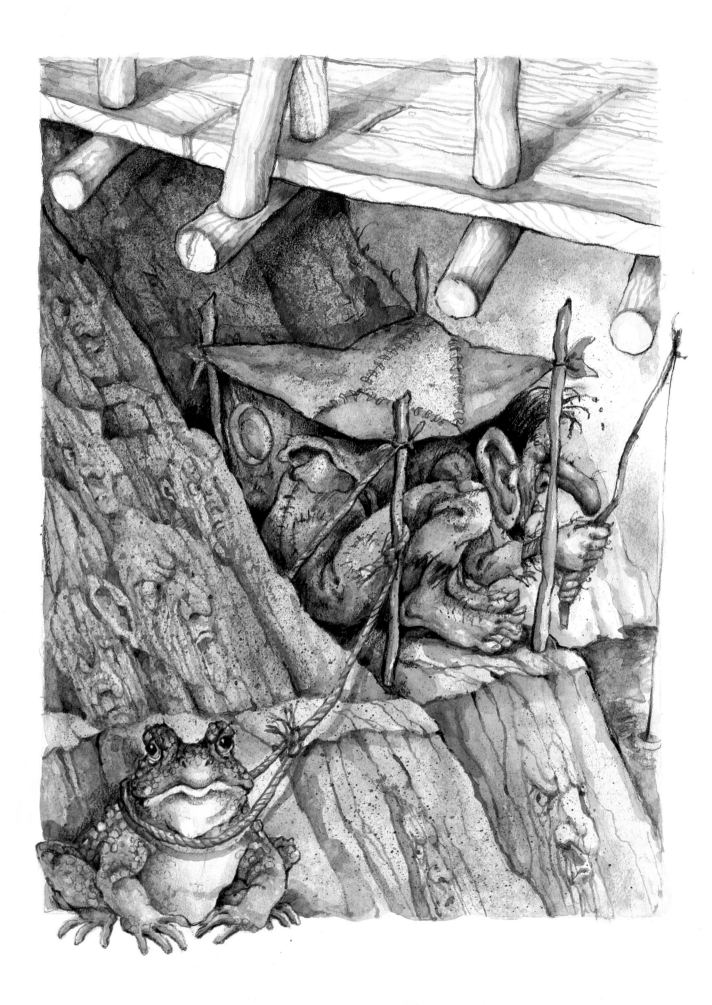

The three Billy Goats Gruff knew that on the hill, beyond the river, grew sweet green grass. But under the bridge lived a great ugly troll with eyes as big as saucers and a nose as long as a poker.

And the troll was hungry, too.

What to do?

Well, first of all came the youngest Billy Goat Gruff to cross the bridge. "Trip, trap, trip, trap!" went the bridge.

"WHO'S THAT TRIPPING OVER MY BRIDGE?" roared the troll.

"Oh, it is only I, the tiniest Billy Goat Gruff, and I'm going up to the hillside to eat the sweet green grass," said the youngest billy goat in a small, small voice.

"Now I'm coming to gobble you up!" said the troll.

"Oh, no! Pray don't take me. I'm too little, that I am," said the billy goat. "Wait a bit till the second Billy Goat Gruff comes. He's much bigger."

"Well! Be off with you, then," said the troll.

A little while after came the second Billy Goat Gruff to cross the bridge. "Trip, trap! Trip, trap! Trip, trap!" went the bridge.

"WHO'S THAT TRIPPING OVER MY BRIDGE?" roared the troll.

"Oh, it's the second Billy Goat Gruff, and I'm going up to the hillside to eat the sweet green grass," said the billy goat, and his voice was not so small.

"Now I'm coming to gobble you up!" said the troll.

"Oh, no! Don't take me. I'm much too thin, that I am. Wait a little till the big Billy Goat Gruff comes. He's much bigger."

"Very well! Be off with you," said the greedy troll.

Just then, up came the big Billy Goat Gruff. "T-r-i-p, t-r-a-p!
T-r-i-p, t-r-a-p! T-r-i-p, t-r-a-p! T-r-i-p, t-r-a-p!" went the
bridge, for the billy goat was so heavy that the bridge creaked
and groaned under him.

"WHO'S THAT TRAMPING OVER MY BRIDGE?" roared the troll.

"It's I! The BIG BILLY GOAT GRUFF!" said the billy goat, who had an ugly hoarse voice of his own.

"NOW I'M COMING TO GOBBLE YOU UP!" roared the troll.

"Well, come along! I've got two spears, four hard hooves, and ugly ears! I've got besides an angry feeling, and I'll poke you and kick you and scare you and send you reeling right off this bridge!"

That was what the billy goat said.

And so he flew at the troll
and poked him and kicked him

and scared him and sent him reeling right off that bridge and
into the river.

Then he went up to the hillside.

There the Billy Goats Gruff ate the sweet green grass, and if they're still hungry, they're still there; and so—

Snip, snap, snout,
This tale's told out.